STEP-BY-STEP EXPERIMENTS WITH MAGNETS

By Gina Hagler

Illustrated by Bob Ostrom

The Child's World

Published by The Child's World®
1980 Lookout Drive • Mankato, MN 56003-1705
800-599-READ • www.childsworld.com

ACKNOWLEDGMENTS
The Child's World®: Mary Berendes, Publishing Director
The Design Lab: Design and production
Red Line Editorial: Editorial direction
Consultant: Dr. Peter Barnes, Assistant Scientist, Astronomy Dept.,
   University of Florida

ISBN 9781609735890
LCCN 2011940144

PHOTO CREDITS
Dana Rothstein/Dreamstime, cover; Pilar Echeverria/Dreamstime, cover,
back cover; Stuart Corlett/Dreamstime, 1, 25; Jim Barber/Shutterstock
Images, 4; Shutterstock Images, 8, 14, 15, 20; Michael Chamberlin/
Shutterstock Images, 17; Patryk Kosmider/Shutterstock Images, 19;
Galushko Sergey/Shutterstock Images, 24

Design elements: Pilar Echeverria/Dreamstime, Robisklp/Dreamstime,
Sarit Saliman/Dreamstime, Jeffrey Van Daele/Dreamstime

Printed in the United States of America

BE SAFE !

The experiments in this book are meant for kids to do themselves. Sometimes an adult's help is needed though. Look in the supply list for each experiment. It will list if an adult is needed. Also, some supplies will need to be bought by an adult.

TABLE OF CONTENTS

4

Magnets can come in fun shapes!

CHAPTER ONE

Study Magnets!

Have you seen a magnet stuck to a refrigerator? Magnets stick to some things, such as metal. But they do not stick to everything.

Magnets have two ends. They are called **poles**. One is its north pole. The other is its south pole. A magnetic **force** pushes or pulls magnets. The magnetic force is strongest at a magnet's poles. Opposite poles of magnets **attract**, or pull together. If the poles are the same, magnets **repel**, or push away from each other.

This push and pull makes magnets useful. Toy trains connect with magnets. Some doors pull closed with magnets. And recycling centers use big magnets to pull metal from large trash piles. How can you learn more about magnets?

CHAPTER TWO

Seven Science Steps

Doing a science **experiment** is a fun way to discover new facts!
An experiment follows steps to find answers to science questions.
This book has experiments to help you learn about magnets.
You will follow the same seven steps in each experiment:

Seven Steps

1. **Research**: Figure out the facts before you get started.
2. **Question**: What do you want to learn?
3. **Guess**: Make a **prediction**. What do you think will happen in the experiment?
4. **Gather**: Find the supplies you need for your experiment.
5. **Experiment**: Follow the directions.
6. **Review**: Look at the results of the experiment.
7. **Conclusion**: The experiment is done. Now it is time to reach a **conclusion**. Was your prediction right?

Are you ready to become a scientist? Let's experiment to learn about magnets!

Can paper clips become magnetized?

8

CHAPTER THREE

Magnet Magic

You can buy many kinds of magnets. Some are shaped in bars. And some have pictures glued to them. Many objects are not magnets, though. Try this to learn if paper clips can become magnets.

Research the Facts

Here are a few. What else do you know?

- Only some things are magnetic. Magnets are usually made of metal.
- A paper clip is made from metal.
- Metal is not always magnetic.

Ask Questions

- Can a magnet make another object magnetic?
- Can metals that are not magnetic become magnets?

Make a Prediction

Here are two examples:

- A magnet can make a paper clip magnetic.
- A magnet cannot make a paper clip magnetic.

Gather Your Supplies!

- Table
- White sheet of paper
- 2 large metal paper clips
- Bar or horseshoe magnet
- Pencil or pen
- Paper

Time to Experiment!

1. Place the white paper on the table.

2. Place one paper clip on the paper.

3. Place the other paper clip on the paper. Put the ends by each other. Make them about 1/4 inch (5 cm) apart.

4. Record what happens.

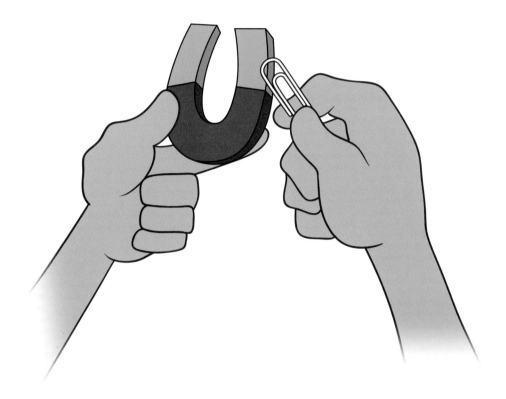

5. Pick up one paper clip. Rub the paper clip on the magnet. Only rub in one direction.

6. Place the paper clip back on the paper.

7. Rub the other paper clip with the magnet. Only rub in one direction.

8. Place the second paper clip back in the same place.

9. Record what happens.

Review the Results

What did you see? Did the paper clips move before they were rubbed on the magnet? Did they move after they were rubbed on the magnet? The paper clips did not move the first time they were placed on the paper. After the paper clips were rubbed on the magnet, they moved closer when on the paper.

What Is Your Conclusion?

The paper clips became magnetic when they were rubbed on the magnet. The paper clips contain iron. Metal with iron can become magnetized.

A paper clip only stays magnetized for a short time. If you rub it longer on the magnet, the paper clip will be magnetic for a longer time.

Paper clips stick together when they are magnetized.

CHAPTER FOUR

Magnetic or Not?

Does everything stick to magnets? Does wood have iron in it? How about plastic? Try this to find out!

Research the Facts

Here are a few. What other facts can you find?

- Magnetic things contain iron.

- Metals are hard and shiny solid objects.

Do magnets attract plastic snap blocks?

15

Ask Questions

- Is wood, a soda pop can, or plastic magnetic?
- Do both poles of a magnet pull toward magnetic things?

Make a Prediction

Here are two examples:

- Plastic and wood are magnetic. They stick to a magnet.
- Plastic and wood are not magnetic. They do not stick to a magnet.

Gather Your Supplies!

- A few plastic snap blocks
- A few pennies
- A few small metal paper clips
- A few wooden toothpicks
- Soda pop can
- Plastic container (large enough to hold everything)
- Bar magnet (with an N and S marking the poles)
- Pencil or pen
- Paper

Magnets have north and south poles.

Time to Experiment!

1. Place the snap blocks, pennies, soda pop can, paper clips, and toothpicks in the container. Mix them around.

2. Move the south pole of the magnet around in the container. Put it close by the objects.

3. Does anything stick to the magnet? Record what happens.

4. Now move the north pole of the magnet over the objects. Record what happens.

Review the Results

Read your notes. Which objects did not pull to the magnet? What were those objects made of? The pennies and paper clips stuck to both poles of the magnet. The snap blocks, soda pop can, and toothpicks did not stick to either poles of the magnet.

What Is Your Conclusion?

The magnet's poles have the same magnetic force. The pennies and the paper clips contain magnetic things. You can tell because they pull toward the magnet. The snap blocks, soda pop can, and toothpicks did not pull. They do not contain magnetic things. Plastic, soda pop cans, and wood are not magnetic.

Magnetic objects have iron, nickel, magnetite, and cobalt in them. A soda pop can is made from aluminum. Aluminum is a metal, but it is not magnetic.

Soda pop cans are made from aluminum.

CHAPTER FIVE

Do Opposites Attract?

Have you felt a toy train's cars pull together? The train has magnets on the end of each car. They attract the other magnets. But sometimes magnets push away. Why does this happen? In this experiment, you will learn why.

A toy train connects with the pull of magnets.

Research the Facts

Here are a few. What other facts do you know?

- Every magnet has a north and a south pole.
- North and south poles are on the opposite ends of a magnet.

Ask Questions

- Do the same poles of two magnets push or pull when touched?
- Do the opposite poles of two magnets push or pull when touched?

Make a Prediction

Here are two examples:

- Opposite poles of two magnets push when put near each other.
- Opposite poles of two magnets pull when put near each other.

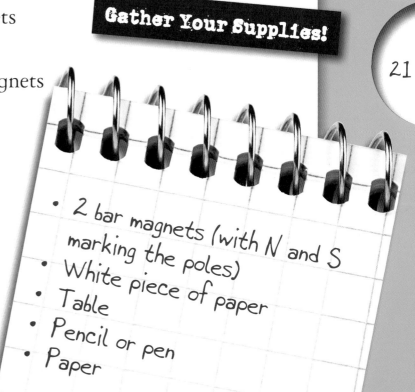

Gather Your Supplies!

- 2 bar magnets (with N and S marking the poles)
- White piece of paper
- Table
- Pencil or pen
- Paper

Time to Experiment!

1. Place the white paper on the table.
2. Place the two bar magnets on the paper. Put them about 1/4 inch (6 cm) apart. Make sure the same poles face each other.
3. Record what happens.
4. Turn one magnet. Make sure the opposite poles face each other.
5. Record what happens.

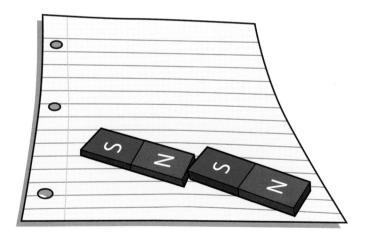

Review the Results

Read your notes. What happened when the opposite poles faced each other? What happened when the same poles faced each other? When the two north or south poles faced each other, the magnets pushed apart. When a north and a south pole faced each other, the magnets pulled together.

What Is Your Conclusion?

Opposite poles on a magnet pull toward each other. Even if you push really hard, the same poles of two magnets will not stick together. The force in a magnet points in one direction. It moves in through the south pole and out the north pole. When a south pole touches a north pole, the forces from each pole work together. They make the poles join. When two of the same poles touch, the forces from each work against each other. They push the poles apart.

A compass helps you find the direction you want to go.

24

CHAPTER SIX

Point the Compass

Many people use compasses to find their way. They look at the needle on the compass to see where it points. Inside a compass is a magnet. Try this experiment to see how a compass works and where it points.

Research the Facts

Here are a few. What other facts do you know?

- Earth has a **magnetic field**. The magnetic field is between the North and South Poles of Earth.
- A compass needle always points in one direction.

Ask Questions

- How does a compass work?
- Why is a magnet used in a compass?

Make a Prediction

Here are two examples:

- A compass needle pulls toward Earth's poles.
- A compass needle does not pull toward Earth's poles.

Gather Your Supplies!

- Adult help
- Bar magnet (with N and S marking the poles)
- A sewing needle
- Bowl
- Wax paper
- Scissors
- Water
- Pencil or pen
- Paper

Time to Experiment!

1. Pour water into the bowl.
2. Cut a circle from the wax paper. Make sure it is small enough to move around in the bowl.
3. Rub one end of the needle on the north pole of the magnet. Rub the needle in one direction, from end to tip. You can ask an adult to help you.

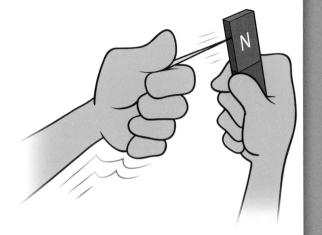

4. Rub the other end of the needle on the south pole of the magnet. Rub the needle in one direction.
5. Stick the needle through the wax paper. Push the tip out again on the same side.
6. Float the wax paper and needle on top of the water in the bowl. Gently spin the paper.

7. Watch what happens. Record what you see.

8. Spin the paper again. Where does it stop this time? Record what you see.

Review the Results

Check out your notes. Did the paper and needle stop spinning? Where did the needle point? Both times, the needle pointed in the same direction.

What Is Your Conclusion?

When a magnet is balanced on something, it will always point to Earth's North and South Poles. The Earth is like a very big magnet. Its force pushes and pulls magnets. The Earth's force goes from its North to South Poles. This makes a compass needle point north.

You are a scientist now. What fun magnet facts did you learn? You found out magnets have opposite poles. You learned that many metals are magnetic. You can learn even more about magnets. Study them. Experiment with them. Then share what you learn about magnets.

Glossary

attract (uh-TRAKT): To attract is to pull toward another object. Opposite poles of magnets attract.

conclusion (kuhn-KLOO-shuhn): A conclusion is what you learn from doing an experiment. One conclusion is that only some metals are magnetic.

experiment (ek-SPER-uh-ment): An experiment is a test or way to study something to learn facts. This experiment showed how a compass works.

force (FORSS): A force is an action that changes an object's shape or how it moves. A force pushes or pulls between magnets.

magnetic field (mag-NET-ik FEELD): A magnetic field is the area around a magnet that has the power to attract other metals. The magnetic field is strong at a magnet's poles.

poles (POHLZ): The opposite ends of a magnet are its poles. Every magnet has two poles.

prediction (pri-DIKT-shun): A prediction is what you think will happen in the future. The prediction about magnets was wrong.

repel (ri-PEL): To repel is to push away. The same poles of a magnet repel each other.

Books

Gibson, Gary. *Playing with Magnets.* Mankato, MN: Stargazer Books, 2010.

Jennings, Terry. *Magnets.* Mankato, MN: A+/Smart Apple Media, 2009.

Vogel, Julia. *Push and Pull! Learn About Magnets.* Mankato, MN: The Child's World, 2011.

Index

32

Web Sites

Visit our Web site for links about magnet experiments:
childsworld.com/links

Note to Parents, Teachers, and Librarians: We routinely verify our Web links to make sure they are safe and active sites. So encourage your readers to check them out!

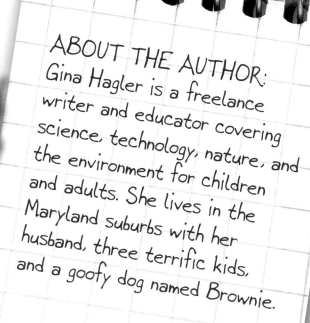

ABOUT THE AUTHOR:
Gina Hagler is a freelance writer and educator covering science, technology, nature, and the environment for children and adults. She lives in the Maryland suburbs with her husband, three terrific kids, and a goofy dog named Brownie.